Our Endangered Planet
LIFE ON LAND

Mary Hoff
and
Mary M. Rodgers

LERNER PUBLICATIONS COMPANY • MINNEAPOLIS

Thanks to Dr. Edward Cushing, James E. Laib, Bill Kauffmann, Zachary Marell, and Gary Hansen for their help in preparing this book.

Words in **bold** type are listed in a glossary that starts on page 66.

LIBRARY OF CONGRESS CATALOGING-IN-PUBLICATION DATA

Hoff, Mary King.
    Our endangered planet. Life on land / Mary Hoff and Mary M. Rodgers.
      p.   cm.
    Includes bibliographical references and index.
    Summary: Describes the delicate ecological balance among all living things on land, the damage done by humanity in contributing to the extinction of various species, and ways of preventing further harm.
    ISBN 0-8225-2507-0 (lib. bdg.)
    1. Extinction (Biology)—Juvenile literature. 2. Man—Influence on nature—Juvenile literature. 3. Endangered species—Juvenile literature. 4. Nature conservation—Juvenile literature. [1. Extinction (Biology) 2. Rare Animals. 3. Rare plants. 4. Man—Influence on nature. 5. Ecology. 6. Wildlife conservation.] I. Rodgers, Mary M. (Mary Madeline), 1954–   . II. Title.
QH78.H64   1992
333.95'137—dc20   91–40960
                                  CIP
                                   AC

Manufactured in the United States of America

1 2 3 4 5 6 7 8 9 10 01 00 99 98 97 96 95 94 93 92

Front cover: A herd of bison (North American buffalo) graze on pasture in the central United States. Back cover: (Left) Enjoying the beauty of a park, children walk hand in hand among golden, leaf-shedding trees. (Right) Garbage litters the ground in Cold Springs, New York.

Recycled paper

All paper used in this book is of recycled material and may be recycled.

Recyclable

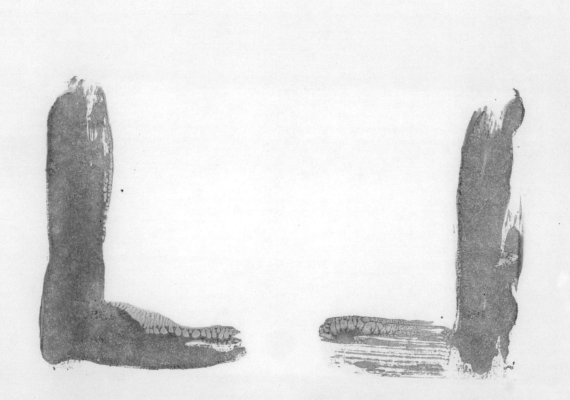

CONTENTS

Our Endangered Planet

In the 1960s, astronauts first traveled beyond the earth's protective atmosphere and were able to look back at our planet. What they saw was a beautiful globe, turning slowly in space. That image reminds us that our home planet has limits, for we know of no other place that can support life.

The various parts of our natural environment—including people, air, water, soil, plants, and animals—are partners in making our planet a good place to live. If we endanger one element, the other partners are badly affected, too.

People throughout the world are working to protect and heal the earth's environment. They recognize that making nature our ally and not our victim is the way to shape a common future. Because we have only one planet to share, its health and survival mean that we all can live.

Our planet holds millions of different kinds of plants and animals. Some live on land, and some live in water. For centuries, this huge group of living things has given us food, medicines, and raw materials. In reaping these benefits, we have exercised strong control over nature. For example, we have uprooted plants and killed animals to make room for other plants and animals that are more useful to us.

Our actions have destroyed the natural homes of many creatures and have produced pollution in the air, water, and soil. These conditions make it difficult—sometimes even impossible—for our partners on the earth to survive.

Laws now protect some living things from further destruction. Groups of people have worked hard to restore the living spaces of some plants and animals. Understanding our role in nature—not as controller but as partner—will help us to ensure that the many different living things on our planet will survive into the twenty-first century.

CHAPTER ONE

THE LIFE POOL

A rich variety of living things surrounds us on our planet. Perhaps right now a leafy plant sits on a shelf near you or a bird sings outside your window or a fly buzzes around your head. Yet, before you go to bed tonight, at least one animal or plant will become **extinct**—meaning that the last individual member of that **species,** or kind, will die.

START HERE!

To discover why and how so many plants and animals are disappearing, we need to figure out how they got here in the first place. Life on earth began about four billion years ago. The first forms of life probably were **bacteria**—tiny plants made up of just a single cell. Cells are the building blocks of all living things. The body of a human being, for example, contains billions of cells.

Inside the cells of its body, each plant and each animal has a set of **genes.** These are units that act as secret codes to define the appearance, behavior, sex, and other features of a specific plant or animal. If you have brown eyes, for example, it is because the code for that trait is written in your genes. Genes are passed from a plant or an animal to its babies—the offspring that form the next generation of that type of plant or animal.

Sometimes, however, a secret code **mutates,** meaning that it changes slightly

(Left) After a rainstorm, the parents of baby cardinals return to the nest to feed their young.

from one generation to the next. As a result, an offspring may have a physical trait that its parents do not have. Over many generations, this slow but sure process of change, often called **evolution,** has helped to create our planet's rich variety of life.

There are roughly 250 different kinds of roses, and growers continue to breed new types.

As creatures evolved, some had genes that helped them to **adapt.** This means that the plant or the animal changed to fit into its **habitat,** or natural surroundings. These animals and plants were more likely to have offspring, passing their genes to the next generation. Plants and animals that did not successfully adapt to their habitat were more likely to die without producing offspring.

THE NUMBERS GAME

How many different types of animals and plants do you think there are on the earth today? Scientists estimate that our planet holds at least 5 million—and maybe up to 30 million—different species of living creatures. But experts have named only 1.5 million species. One million of the known species are insects!

Remember, these are entirely different species of butterflies, trees, and frogs—not the individual members of the species. Our planet may have a million members of one species of frog and just a hundred of another kind of frog, but we are still talking about only two species of frog.

Most of the living things on our planet belong to one of two groups—plants or animals. Plants, which include grass, flowers, and trees, make their own food from sunlight, water, and chemicals. Animals, such as birds, fish, humans, and insects, depend on other living things—plants or other animals—for the food they need to survive.

LIFE ON LAND

Our planet has many different kinds of habitats, each of which contains a unique blend of plants and animals. One of the most obvious divisions in habitat types is between those on land and those in water. The focus in this book is on **terrestrial** (land-based) plants and animals.

Differences exist even among terrestrial habitats. The desert, for example, supports plants and animals that have adapted to dry conditions. Tropical rain forests contain species that thrive in a moist, warm

Camels are ideally suited to life in the desert because they can go without water for many days. Their humps store fat—not water—for use as energy when food is scarce.

This golden-haired tamarin, a kind of monkey, lives in the tropical rain forests of Central and South America.

environment. In polar regions, such as in Alaska or Greenland, animals and plants that can stand very cold weather have evolved.

Some habitats support a greater variety of creatures than others do. Tropical rain forests, which encircle the earth near the equator, are crowded with living things. Scientists have estimated that, in a 25-square-mile (65-square-kilometer) plot of rain forest, we could count 1,500 kinds of flowering plants. But in all of Antarctica— the huge, ice-covered continent at the southern end of our planet—only two kinds of flowering plants exist.

Thousands of kinds of plants and animals—from broad-leafed trees to tiny insects—crowd the world's rain forests.

Dinosaurs ate either vegetation or other dinosaurs. These animals became extinct millions of years ago—before humans lived on our planet. Scientists are still trying to figure out the most likely explanation for the dinosaurs' disappearance.

A NATURAL CHANGE

In the flow of life on earth, species come and go. When habitats change, the kinds of animals and plants that adapt best to the new conditions survive. Over many generations, some types may even evolve into new species. At the same time, other species may be unable to live under the changed conditions and may become extinct.

Since life began, hundreds of thousands of creatures have disappeared. During the great dinosaur die-off, which happened about 65 million years ago, roughly one-fourth of all the species then on our planet became extinct. But many life-forms—including some types of turtles and lizards—survived and are the ancestors of the creatures around us today.

A TASTE OF TAXONOMY
Part I—Seven-Up

Have you ever wondered how scientists keep track of the huge variety of plants and animals on our planet? Only slight differences may distinguish one species from another, but each species needs a separate name. The science of naming and classifying plants and animals is called **taxonomy.**

Scientists have created two similar systems of classification, one for plants and one for animals. Each system first groups living things by what they have in common and then gradually sorts them by their differences.

Taxonomists use seven main categories of sorting. The largest grouping in the plant and the animal systems is the **kingdom.** The animal kingdom—Animalia—has about one million named members, and the plant kingdom—Plantae—contains about 350,000. The animal kingdom is then divided into **phyla** and the plant kingdom into **divisions.** For example, all plants that have flowers belong to the same division.

Members of a plant or an animal **class** have basic traits in common. **Mammals,** for instance, are a class of animals that produce milk to feed their young. Next is the **order** of plant or animal, which indicates other, more specific common traits. Among mammals, some eat flesh, others eat plants, and still others eat insects. Each of these orders has its own name.

Identifying a **family** of plant or animal helps us sort through even more characteristics. For example, flesh-eating mammals with long noses and bushy tails are in the same family. Within a **genus,** the members are very alike. They may look and act similar, but some differences still exist. Although coyotes and timberwolves are in the same genus, they cannot breed with one another.

Species, the narrowest category of classification, is the most specific kind of living thing. Members of the same species can breed, and their offspring look like the parents.

The Michigan lily [Lilium michiganense] *flourishes in the grasslands not only of Michigan but of several other U.S. midwestern states.*

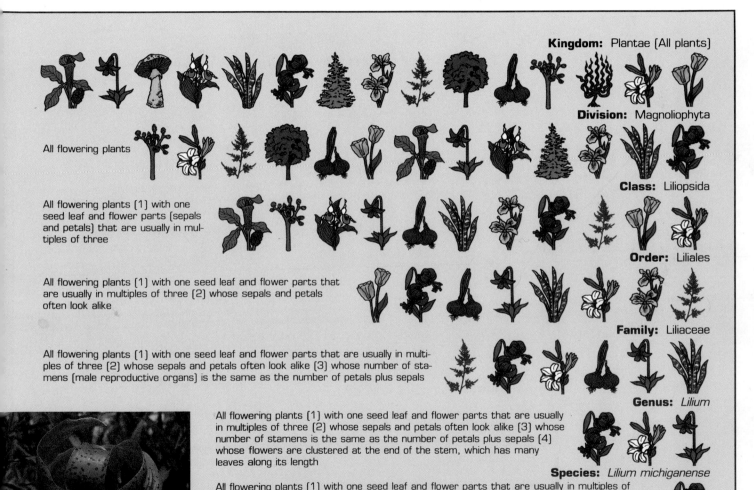

Kingdom: Plantae [All plants]

Division: Magnoliophyta

All flowering plants

Class: Liliopsida

All flowering plants [1] with one seed leaf and flower parts [sepals and petals] that are usually in multiples of three

Order: Liliales

All flowering plants [1] with one seed leaf and flower parts that are usually in multiples of three [2] whose sepals and petals often look alike

Family: Liliaceae

All flowering plants [1] with one seed leaf and flower parts that are usually in multiples of three [2] whose sepals and petals often look alike [3] whose number of stamens [male reproductive organs] is the same as the number of petals plus sepals

Genus: *Lilium*

All flowering plants [1] with one seed leaf and flower parts that are usually in multiples of three [2] whose sepals and petals often look alike [3] whose number of stamens is the same as the number of petals plus sepals [4] whose flowers are clustered at the end of the stem, which has many leaves along its length

Species: *Lilium michiganense*

All flowering plants [1] with one seed leaf and flower parts that are usually in multiples of three [2] whose sepals and petals often look alike [3] whose number of stamens is the same as the number of petals plus sepals [4] whose flowers are clustered at the end of the stem, which has many leaves along its length [5] whose flowers point downward with the sepals and petals curled backward

CHAPTER TWO

NATURE'S BALANCE

In the world of nature, there is no such thing as surviving on your own. Bacteria, for example, help cows to digest food. Grass benefits from the work of earthworms that burrow through the soil, preparing it for the grass's roots. Fruit-bearing rain-forest trees shelter and nourish tropical birds. As they search flowers for food, honeybees collect and carry the **pollen** of the plant (a fine dust) on their legs. Flying from one flower to another, the bees

(Left) A honeybee gathers nectar (sweet juice) from the colorful center of a sunflower. The sugar-filled nectar is the raw material that the insect needs to make honey. The bee's legs are covered with pollen—the fine dust that the sunflower needs to make new plants. As partners in the web of life, the honeybee and the sunflower help one another to survive and reproduce.

pollinate—an action that is needed for new seeds to form.

THE WEB OF LIFE

Living things depend on one another so much that scientists describe the way they interact as the **web of life.** Because we are all connected in the web of life, when a single species becomes extinct it is not the only species affected. Scientists estimate that the extinction of one plant may cause up to 30 other species of plants and animals to disappear, too. The same thing happens when an animal becomes extinct. Let's look at a specific example of this change.

The dodo was a flightless bird that once lived on the island of Mauritius, which lies off the coast of eastern Africa in the

We know about the dodo bird, which has been extinct since the late 1600s, because of drawings that explorers made of the bird and because of bones preserved in museums.

Indian Ocean. In the seventeenth century, European explorers landed on the island. These adventurers—and the non-native animals they brought with them—found the dodo birds easy to kill because they could not fly. The newcomers hunted the dodo to extinction.

After the dodo was gone, the dodo tree, a native Mauritian plant, was in trouble. Since the dodo's extinction, no new dodo trees have sprouted on the island without scientific help. A researcher recently discovered the reason. Dodos ate the dodo trees' nuts and digested the hard shells. This action allowed the seeds to sprout. Without dodos, the seeds were trapped in the nutshells and could no longer become new plants. Until scientists found ways to free the seeds, the dodo tree faced extinction.

A TASTE OF TAXONOMY
Part II—The Name Game

Scientists classify animals and plants in systems with seven groups—kingdom, phylum or division, class, order, family, genus, and species. Now let's look at actual names.

The easy names by which we identify plants and animals—English oak tree or California condor, for example—are known as common names. A plant or an animal can have dozens of common names, depending on languages and regions throughout the world. In the 1700s, the Swedish scientist Carolus Linnaeus came up with a flexible, scientific method for listing every species. Thanks to this system, scientists from China to Brazil use the same scientific name to talk about the same species.

Scientific names appear in Latin or Greek —languages that early scholars used. Most of the time, when you see a scientific name, it is in a slanted type called italic. The first part of the name is the genus, which is capitalized. In the case of oak trees, the genus is *Quercus*. For condors, the genus is *Gymnogyps*.

The second part of the name is the species. For example, an English oak tree is *Quercus robur,* and a California condor is *Gymnogyps californianus.*

The species name has no capital letters and often portrays a characteristic or location of this particular kind of living thing. *Eleutherodactylus portoricensis,* which translates roughly as "free-fingered Puerto Rican one," describes a tiny frog from Puerto Rico whose toes are not webbed together.

In some cases, the species name may honor a person who found or studied the species. Even political figures have had plants or animals scientifically named after them. *Ornithoptera alexandrae* (Queen Alexandra's birdwing butterfly), for instance, is named for a British queen of the early 1900s.

A member of the species Eleutherodactylus portoricensis *clings to a leaf.*

THE PEOPLE CONNECTION

Humans depend on plants and animals for survival, too. Plants, while producing their own food, make the oxygen we need to breathe. Plants also provide wood for furniture and paper for books. Breads, rice, and breakfast cereals come from the grains we grow. People use the fluff from cotton plants to make some of our clothes. Vegetables are plain, ordinary plants, and fruits are the seed-bearing parts of flowering plants! Plants beautify a walk in a shady wood or cushion a tumble on a grassy soccer field.

Materials used in industries—such as rubbers, gums, soaps, dyes, and resins—come from plants. The roots of some plants keep our water clean by holding down soil that otherwise would wash into rivers and streams. Other plants absorb the poisonous gases that are part of air pollution.

Let's not forget animals, which give us meat, eggs, and milk products. Wool from sheep and silk spun by silkworms provide us with raw material for clothing. In many parts of the world, people depend on animals for transportation, for plowing fields, and for running simple machinery.

Two teams of young soccer players practice their skills on a grassy field in Zimbabwe, a country in southern Africa.

These are just some of the ways that plants and animals help us live. We also rely on them for medicines. For example, the leaves of a flower called the rosy periwinkle are the raw material for an anti-cancer agent. An Asian shrub named the

An Australian shearer shaves the fleece (coat of wool) from a medium-haired sheep. The fleece, which is processed into wool products, grows back within a year and can be clipped again.

Farmers in the Philippine Islands of southeastern Asia sink rice plants in a water-filled plot called a paddy.

serpentine root helps to treat dysentery, cholera, and other diseases. In small amounts, poison from the Malayan pit viper, a deadly snake, prevents blood clots from forming in human blood.

The list is nearly endless and reminds us that we humans cannot survive alone. We depend on the web of life just as much as any other animal or plant does. When it comes to life, "we are all in this together."

CHAPTER THREE

DEAD AS A DODO

Have you ever had a good friend move away from you? If you have, you know what it is like to lose someone who is very important in your life. You cannot do the things you used to do—at least not in the same way. Your world has changed.

Today, somewhere on the globe, our world will lose a plant or animal that is the last of its species. That loss will tear a hole in the web of life. The plants and animals—including people—that depended on the extinct species will have to turn elsewhere, if they can, for what they need to survive.

ON FULL BLAST

Although extinctions are part of the natural flow of life on our planet, they are occurring faster than ever before. If past

(Left) **Wildlife rangers have piled up the skins of animals that were poached in Brazil. Poaching has endangered the survival of many of our planet's cat species.** *(Above)* **"Martha," the world's last passenger pigeon, died in an Ohio zoo in 1914. In the 1800s, millions of the birds flew over the central United States.**

Throughout the twentieth century, our actions—from polluting the air with auto fumes (left) to increasing the planet's human population (right)—have caused a rise in rates of extinction.

extinctions were a dripping faucet, they now are a faucet that is on full blast. Between the years 1600 and 1900, **mammals** (warm-blooded animals that nurse their young) and birds became extinct at a rate of about one species every four years. During the first half of the 1900s, the rate rose to one species per year.

By the 1970s, researchers were estimating that our world was losing one species of plant or animal *every day!* And some experts say that by 2000, extinctions will skyrocket to 100 per day. That is one species of plant or animal every 15 minutes— the time it takes to eat a quick breakfast. Some scientists predict that half of all of the species now in the world will have disappeared by 2050.

The faster rate of extinctions is the result of two human factors—the increasing number of people on our planet and our treatment of the global environment. Let's

look at some of the ways in which people force animals and plants to the edge of extinction—and over it.

NO PLACE TO CALL HOME

Most of the harm we do to other species results from destroying their habitats. As our planet's population has grown, we have cleared forests and grasslands, have drained swamps, and have even watered deserts. These actions enabled us to make more farmland, to create more towns, and to build more factories. The losers in this changeover are the plants and animals that once inhabited those spaces.

The destruction of tropical rain forests is the most threatening example of habitat loss on our planet. Although they cover less than 10 percent of the world's land surface, these forests contain more than half of the world's species. Developers are harvesting the trees to sell, and farmers are cutting and burning vegetation to make farmland.

Madagascar, a tropical island off the coast of eastern Africa, once had more than

30 species of lemurs. These monkeylike animals are found nowhere else in the world. But the human population of Madagascar is growing fast, and food is scarce. Farmers have cleared more than 90 percent of the lemurs' habitat, and 14 of the species have become extinct.

Many rain-forest plants and animals have helped humankind. Yet developers and farmers are wiping out roughly 100 acres (40 hectares) of these forests *every minute.* This area is the same as 77 football fields. Scientists estimate that a handful of species is becoming extinct daily. We can only imagine what benefits we have lost by destroying these unique environments.

A sifaka lemur clings to a tree in Madagascar, a large tropical island near eastern Africa.

To create farmland, workers cut and burn rain forests to clear away native vegetation. This practice has caused the loss of thousands of tropical species that make their homes in the forests.

TERRESTRIAL TITANS

THE NOISIEST ANIMAL: the howling monkey of Central and South America, whose scream can be heard 10 miles [16 kilometers] away.

THE FASTEST-GROWING PLANT: a variety of lily in the British Isles that grew 12 feet [3.6 meters] in 14 days in 1978.

THE STRONGEST ANIMAL: the rhinoceros beetle, which can support 850 times its own weight. This is the equivalent of a 100-pound [45-kilogram] sixth-grader lifting 43 tons [39 metric tons].

THE TALLEST PLANT: a redwood tree in California that rises to 362 feet [110 meters].

A redwood tree reaches toward the sunlight in northern California.

THE RAREST PLANT: the last member of *Pennantia baylisiana.* It lives on an island in the South Pacific and cannot bear fruit [reproduce] because no other *Pennantia* exists to pollinate it.

THE SLEEPIEST ANIMAL: a tie between an armadillo, an opossum, and a sloth, each of which can sleep or doze about 80 percent of every day.

THE OLDEST PLANT: "King Clone," a creosote plant living in southwestern California that is estimated to be nearly 12,000 years old.

THE HUNGRIEST ANIMAL: a larva [young insect] of the *Polyphemus* moth of North America that eats 86,000 times its own weight within the first two months of life. This is similar to a 7-pound [3-kilogram] human baby eating about 300 tons [272 metric tons] of food in 60 days.

DIRECT HIT

The most obvious way we threaten plants and animals with destruction is by over-hunting or overharvesting them. People have always hunted for food. It is only recently, however, that we have used machine guns, airplanes, jeeps, and other high-tech equipment. These modern meth-

Shooting bison (North American buffalo) from trains was a popular sport in the 1800s. Millions of the animals once roamed the plains of the central United States. By the early 1900s, only a few hundred were left. Conservation efforts have increased the total number of bison in North America to about 20,000.

ods do not give the animal a chance to escape. They also allow us to kill large numbers of animals at a time.

In addition, more people are hunting for sport or for furs, hides, feathers, and other decorations instead of for food. Animals often are hunted wastefully. Elephant and rhinoceros hunters, for example, usually cut out the animals' valuable ivory tusks and leave the rest of the carcass to rot.

Some **poachers** (people who hunt wildlife illegally) in North America kill black bears for their gallbladders and claws. Bear gallbladders, which many Asians use as medicine, fetch high prices.

Some rich people pay poachers to kill certain animals for their heads and antlers, which can be mounted as trophies. Many species of big cats are sacrificed for their

A poacher in southern Africa cut out the valuable ivory tusk of this white rhinoceros and left the rest of the dead animal to rot.

pelts (coats). Furriers (people who make furs) need the pelts of roughly 15 to 25 endangered ocelots or snow leopards or cheetahs to make one fur coat.

Even plants can be overhunted. We can no longer enjoy the red, sweet-smelling sandalwood tree of the Juan Fernández Islands off South America's Pacific coast. Woodcarvers and other artisans liked the wood so much they cut down all the islands' sandalwood trees. Cactuses from Mexico are in trouble because they are being torn from their habitats in huge numbers to be used as houseplants.

A young ocelot (above) plays with the feather of a macaw parrot. Ocelot skins (right) hang from a porch in Ecuador, South America. The ocelot is one of South America's most endangered cat species.

PEOPLE POISON

Some animals have come close to extinction from people-made poisons, such as **pesticides** (chemicals that kill unwanted insects and other pests). Even if these dangerous substances do not kill a species outright, they may weaken it so that it can easily be hunted or is unable to reproduce.

In the 1970s, for example, bird watchers noticed a decline in the number of bald eagles, peregrine falcons, and California condors. These experts eventually traced the cause to **dichloro-diphenyl-tri-chloroethane (DDT).** Planes sprayed this pesticide on farmland and cities to get rid of insects. Over time, DDT became stored in the bodies of small birds and other animals eaten by the larger birds of prey.

As a result, DDT also got into the bodies of the falcons, condors, and eagles. The pesticide made the birds' eggshells so thin that they would break before the baby birds were old enough to hatch. A ban on the use of DDT is helping these large birds to make a comeback.

A plane sprays deadly chemicals on a field to kill insects that harm plants. The pesticide, however, can also hurt other living things by polluting water sources, by poisoning soil, or by being consumed by plant-eating animals.

Many people believe that air pollution—much of it caused by the fumes from our cars, factories, and furnaces—is making the world's weather warmer. A permanent shift in temperature or in the amount of rainfall could affect food sources by changing living conditions for certain kinds of animals and plants. These species may be unable to survive in the new climate of their habitats.

In addition to changing the weather, air pollution is part of another global problem that affects plants and animals—**acid rain.** The polluting chemicals that come from our cars and smokestacks combine with the water vapor in our atmosphere. The chemicals and water form acid solu-

Pollutants from factory smokestacks (below), combined with water in the air, form acid solutions. These mixtures return to the earth in rainfall. The acid rain damages plants (right) that need clean water to survive and flourish.

tions, which fall back to the earth in rain. Plants are particularly sensitive to acid rain, which has damaged many forests around the world.

UNWANTED NEIGHBORS

The plants and animals that naturally originate, grow, and reproduce in a certain region are called **indigenous** (native)

species. Many indigenous species of plants and animals are threatened with extinction because humans have introduced non-native plants and animals into delicately balanced habitats. The new species may eat the indigenous species or may compete for the food, nesting areas, and space that the native animals and plants need to survive.

This problem is especially serious on islands, because the threatened plants and animals cannot easily travel to a safer habitat. They are faced with a "succeed or die" situation. On New Zealand's North and South islands, for example, non-native species endanger half of the indigenous plants and animals.

Let's look at one more example—the Hawaiian Islands—the only U.S. state with tropical rain forests. When settlers from Europe and North America arrived 200 years ago, the Hawaiian Islands boasted at least 43 native bird species and thousands of indigenous plants.

The newcomers brought cattle, goats, horses, rats, and other foreign animals that ate the native plants, killed the local birds,

The flightless kiwi bird of New Zealand—an island nation in the South Pacific Ocean—once faced extinction but is now protected by law. At one time, the Maori, New Zealand's first settlers, decorated ceremonial cloaks with kiwi feathers. European immigrants to New Zealand later used the bird's hollow legs for pipestems and cooked its flesh in meat pies.

and upset the natural environment. The new people also cleared the rain forests to create farmland, plantations, and ranches.

You can probably guess the result—15 of Hawaii's indigenous bird species are now

The silversword plant—so named because its spiny leaves look like sword points—lives only in the craters of Hawaii's dead volcanoes.

Many native Hawaiian species have become endangered or extinct through the creation of cattle ranches, dairy farms, pineapple plantations, and sugarcane estates.

extinct, and another 19 are quickly disappearing. About 10 percent of the 1,250 native flowering species are lost forever, and another 40 percent are in serious danger of extinction.

THE SPICE OF LIFE

Species extinctions weaken the web of life. They upset the cycle of eating, sheltering, and reproducing on which all of nature depends. Increases in extinctions put more and more strain on the web of life. If the web becomes too weak, it may not hold together.

Species extinctions also affect our planet's **diversity** (variety). Scientists usually describe diversity in two ways. **Biodiversity** refers to the many different kinds of living things on our planet. Within a single species, scientists talk about **genetic diversity.** This is the variety of traits within the genes of the species. These traits help the species to adapt to new situations.

The thick rain forests of Indonesia—a large, populous country in eastern Asia—contain some of the most biologically varied habitats on our planet.

When the population of a species becomes smaller, the genetic diversity of the species becomes smaller, too.

The aisle of fruits and vegetables in a grocery store shows us just a tiny bit of our planet's biodiversity. A look at the people around you illustrates the genetic diversity of the species *Homo sapiens* (human beings). Both types of diversity help to ensure that life can continue as the earth's habitats change through natural and people-made activities.

Local healers on Madagascar taught researchers about the medical benefits of the rosy periwinkle. The little flower's leaves have since helped to extend the life spans of many young cancer patients.

WHY CARE?

Humankind dominates the global environment. We actively—and often negatively—influence the ability of plants and animals to survive and flourish. Because we share this planet with other forms of life, we need to rethink our behavior. We ought not to push our way through existence, bullying the rest of the creatures on the earth.

It may be hard for us to see the value of any one species. But what if we had lost the rosy periwinkle? We would also have lost the anti-cancer drug in its leaves, and many cancer victims would have died. The trees on our planet—in rain forests, in national parks, in backyards, and in countless other spots—help to absorb some of the air pollution we create.

In addition to their usefulness, plants and animals are important sources of beauty and fun. The next time you walk in a wooded park or hear a bird sing or watch the playful antics of your pet, remember that these species enrich our lives just by existing.

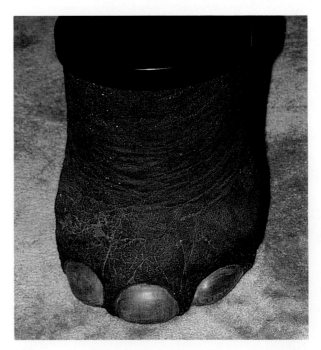

Human use of animals and plants sometimes borders on abuse. This small table has been made from the hollowed-out leg of an elephant.

We need our partners in the web of life, and they need us. But even if we do not benefit directly from other species, many people believe these living things have as much right to be here as we do. By taking actions that force them toward extinction, we are violating that right.

The affection and playfulness of our family pets contributes to our own quality of life.

CHAPTER FOUR

THE PATH TO EXTINCTION

Extinction is usually a gradual process. Conservationists, people who work to save species and habitats, have created categories to describe where a plant or an animal is along the path to extinction. The most common categories are **rare, vulnerable, endangered,** and **extinct.**

To illustrate these different categories, let's imagine a road on which plants and animals travel as they move toward extinction. The road is like any other pathway, except that this one ends at a cliff. Any plant or animal that falls over Extinction Cliff is gone forever.

THE FIRST STOP

We will start our trip by visiting a few rare species. These are plants and animals that exist in limited numbers. They are not on the direct path to extinction, but they easily could be pushed that way because our planet has so few of them.

(Left) A drawing shows rare, vulnerable, and endangered species traveling on the path to extinction. (Above) The ashy dogweed plant may become extinct by 1995. Now found only in Texas, it has lost its living space to industrial developments and housing projects.

37

Lying about 600 miles (965 kilometers) west of Ecuador, South America, the Galápagos Islands contain many wonderful animals that are found nowhere else on earth. Among the region's rare species is the Galápagos flightless cormorant. Roughly 700 pairs of the birds survive along 226 miles (364 kilometers) of narrow coastline.

Crayfish, which these swimming and diving birds catch as their main food, are now being netted in large quantities by

The Galápagos flightless cormorant (above)—a rare bird that lives only on Ecuador's Galápagos Islands—has a limited habitat in the Atlantic Ocean. Fishing crews (left) that haul in large catches of the bird's food are also changing the environmental setting for this species.

Found only in the English county of Gloucester-shire, the adder's tongue spearwort is a rare type of buttercup. Trampling the soil that holds the spearwort's seeds is essential to the growth of the plant.

commercial fishing crews. The small range of the cormorants' habitat and a decreasing food supply make the species extremely sensitive to change.

The adder's tongue spearwort, a tiny yellow flowering plant, is found in just two places, both of them in Britain. More than 50 years ago, a British nature lover set aside land so that this flower could thrive. Few other plants grew in the area, which remained quiet and undisturbed by humans and other animals. Oddly enough, the spearwort did not flourish in its protected habitat.

After many years, scientists figured out that the reason the spearwort was not reproducing was that its habitat *needed* to be disturbed—at least a little—for the plant to sprout. So people trampled the grass in part of the protected area, and the next year thousands of spearworts bloomed. The plant is still considered rare, however, because a local disaster could completely destroy the two spots where this tiny plant lives.

Scientists also consider many of the tropical tree species on the Atlantic coast of Brazil to be rare. Examples of rare animals include the giant ibis of southeastern Asia and the woolly flying squirrel of southern Asia.

A LOOMING THREAT

Vulnerable species are a bit closer to Extinction Cliff than rare species are. In the United States, the term *threatened* is sometimes used to describe vulnerable animals or plants.

The Utah prairie dog—so named because it lives on the prairies (grasslands) of Utah and barks as a warning—is really a vulnerable species of rodent. In the 1800s, when ranchers first started to raise livestock in south central Utah, millions of Utah prairie dogs inhabited the area. They dug holes in the prairie to establish underground burrows, and they fed on the local grass.

The livestock tripped over the burrows, and the prairie dogs competed with the ranchers' cattle and sheep for nourishment. The U.S. government saw the dogs as enemies of ranchers and began a widespread program to poison the animals.

Herds of sheep (right) in Utah compete with Utah prairie dogs (inset right) for food and living space. A drawing (far right) shows the complex underground burrows in which the prairie dogs live.

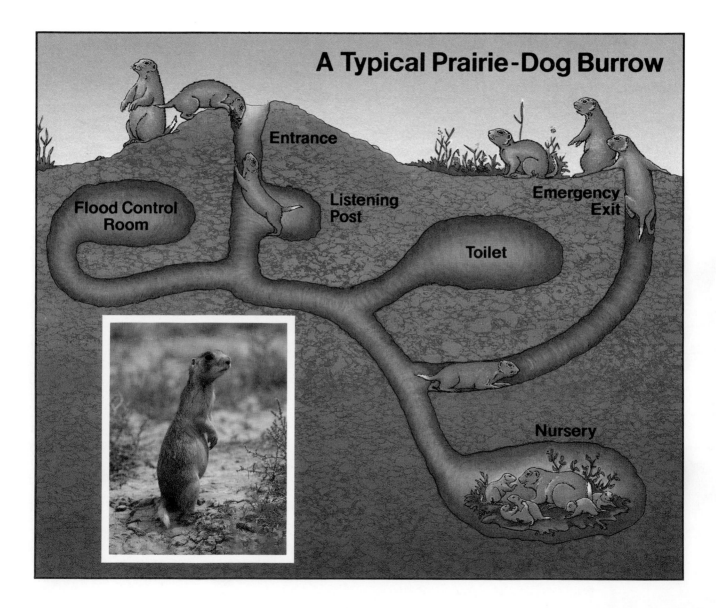

A Typical Prairie-Dog Burrow

By the 1970s, the number of Utah prairie dogs had dropped to about 5,000, and the species was put on the endangered list. But local people pressed for change, and the government began a new program to preserve the dogs. By 1983, there were enough Utah prairie dogs to move the species from the endangered category to the vulnerable group.

The insect-eating tropical pitcher plant—known to scientists as *Nepenthes raja*—is another species on the vulnerable list. This fascinating plant, which grows on the island of Borneo in southeastern Asia, has a deep, pitcher-shaped "mouth" at the end of long vines. The "lips" are smeared with a sweet liquid that attracts insects, which then fall into the mouth to be digested. Covering the pitcher's mouth is a lid.

Nepenthes raja is the largest pitcher plant known to scientists. Because of this quality, people who collect unusual plants pay high prices to buy one. But they have bought the plant almost out of existence. To protect the *Nepenthes raja* from extinction, many countries have agreed to stop

The insect-eating genus Nepenthes—*commonly known as the pitcher plant—has several species, but all of its members have roughly the same shape and feeding habits.*

imports and exports unless special permission is granted.

The threat of extinction looms over other vulnerable animals and plants. Threatened animals include the wood turtle and grizzly bear of the United States, the African elephant, the red kangaroo of Australia, and the tarsier (a small mammal) of the Philippine Islands. Among plants listed as vulnerable are the Mesa Verde cactus of Colorado, the pitcher's thistle of Canada, and the dwarf lake iris of Michigan.

THE DOWNHILL SLIDE

Endangered plants and animals are traveling full speed down the road to extinction. Unless we put up roadblocks by doing something to help them, these species are likely to plunge over Extinction Cliff.

Among our planet's vulnerable species are the tarsier (left) of the Philippine rain forests and the Mesa Verde cactus (right) of Colorado.

Collectors prize the Queen Alexandra's birdwing butterfly—the largest species of butterfly in the world—for its size and vibrant coloring.

Queen Alexandra's birdwing is an endangered species of butterfly. This beautiful insect lives in the lowland rain forests of Papua New Guinea, a tropical nation in southeastern Asia. The largest butterfly in the world, the Queen Alexandra's birdwing measures up to 10 inches (25 centimeters) from wingtip to wingtip.

In the past, the butterfly's unusual size made it very popular with collectors. In modern times, widespread logging of the animal's rain-forest habitat is a much bigger threat. Unless the habitat of the Queen Alexandra's birdwing is protected, this unique insect will exist only as a dead specimen in a butterfly collection.

You probably have seen an African violet, a popular houseplant with bright purple flowers. In the wild, however, the African violet is among the most endangered plants in the world. It is found only in the forests of the Usambara Highlands of eastern Africa.

Workers have cut down parts of the Usambara forest to make farmland and to

Tiny purple flowers distinguish the wild African violet from other vegetation in the Usambara Highlands of eastern Africa.

harvest logs. These actions spell disaster for the wild African violet. Conservationists are trying to protect the plant's habitat. If they fail, the only African violets we will see may be the ones in little clay pots around the house.

The list of endangered plants is long and includes the ashy dogweed of Texas, the Bariaco mahogany tree of Puerto Rico, and the Na'u gardenia of Hawaii. Thousands of animal species are also endangered. Among them are the chimpanzee of Africa, the whooping crane of the United States, the Nile crocodile of Africa and the Middle East, and Przewalski's wild horse of China.

OVER THE EDGE

Would you like to see a moa, a bird that stood 10 feet (3 meters) tall? How about a quagga, a South African animal that appeared to be half-horse and half-zebra? Lots of people would! But we never will, because these extinct species are gone forever.

Colorful drawings are all that remain of male and female huia birds. Found only in New Zealand, they had become extinct by the early 1900s.

Members of the extinct huia species—a black, crow-sized bird from New Zealand —had trouble getting food by themselves.

The male huia had a short, straight bill that was perfect for tapping on trees to shake up the insects inside. But the bill could not get to the insects. The female had a long, curved bill that reached the insects but was useless for tapping. So, for a pair of huias to eat, some serious teamwork was needed!

The Maori, the earliest settlers of New Zealand, hunted huias for their beautiful black-and-white tail feathers. Europeans captured the birds for the unusual shape of their bills. These actions had caused the huia to become extinct by the early 1900s.

During the 1800s, hunters harvested seals and whales in the ocean around Antarctica. Some of the islands in the region, such as the Falklands, became supply stations for hunters. These sites eventually hosted permanent populations of farmers and herders.

The newcomers introduced non-native animals, such as sheep, goats, and rabbits, to the Falklands. The animals grazed on a highly nutritious indigenous grass called *Poa flabellata* until all traces of it were eliminated from the islands. No seeds of this grass were collected, and the rich pasture was lost forever.

These are just two examples of the many species that have fallen over Extinction Cliff. Others include the passenger pigeon of North America, Grey's wallaby of Australia, and the flowering Hau Kuahiwi tree of Hawaii. No matter how we try, we cannot bring back an extinct plant or animal. If we act fast enough, however, we can save the rare, vulnerable, and endangered species that remain.

Sheep graze on the Falkland Islands near southern South America. The animals are not indigenous (native) but arrived with settlers in the 1800s. A local grass became the main food of early herds, which ate the nourishing plants until none was left. Ranchers planted other grasses to replace the extinct native species.

CHAPTER FIVE

FIGHTING FOR LIFE

The web of life is full of holes, but there is time to mend them. People all over the world are working together to help preserve other species. Let's look at some of the ways in which governments, private groups, and ordinary individuals are fighting for life.

CONSERVATION IN ACTION

The most important way we can help to save plants and animals from extinction is to preserve the habitats in which they live. Many organizations protect and restore

(Left) Our planet's population of Bengal tigers was once as low as a few hundred. Through the work of conservation organizations, this cat species did not proceed farther along the path to extinction and now numbers in the thousands.

habitats. These groups may act only at the local level, by preserving a regional wilderness area. Others have an international program that tries to protect many different types of environments around the world.

Founded in 1948, the International Union for the Conservation of Nature (IUCN) keeps track of rare, vulnerable, and endangered species. The IUCN publishes lists of species that are in danger of extinction and suggests ways to save them.

The World Wildlife Fund (WWF) raises money to help preserve endangered species. In the 1970s, for example, the WWF launched Operation Tiger to save the few hundred Bengal tigers that lived in India. Because of the WWF's efforts, more than 3,000 Bengal tigers now roam India's wilderness reserves.

Groups around the world work to protect and preserve endangered species and habitats. (Above left) Marchers show their support for the goals of the late Chico Mendes, who sought to save the Amazon rain forests of Brazil. (Below left) Protesters express their views at a meeting in Antarctica. They want the vast, icy continent to become an internationally protected park. The words Non à la piste mean "No to the runway" and refer to the building of a proposed airplane runway that would disturb breeding penguins. (Above right) Environmental groups also fund scientific research, in this case at a facility in Costa Rica.

Another international group that preserves habitats is the United Nations Educational, Scientific, and Cultural Organization (UNESCO). It runs a program called Man and the Biosphere (MAB).

All over the world, MAB creates **biosphere reserves** (protected wildlife areas) within existing habitats. The program also teaches local groups and governments how to use these natural habitats

The United Nations, an international agency, came up with the idea of biosphere reserves. In these protected zones, people combine the production of foods and other goods with strict conservation methods. The inner core area is reserved for native plants and animals and cannot be disturbed. Surrounding the core are buffer zones for human use, where tourism, food gathering, and scientific research take place. Biosphere reserves offer a way for people and endangered natural habitats to live in harmony with one another.

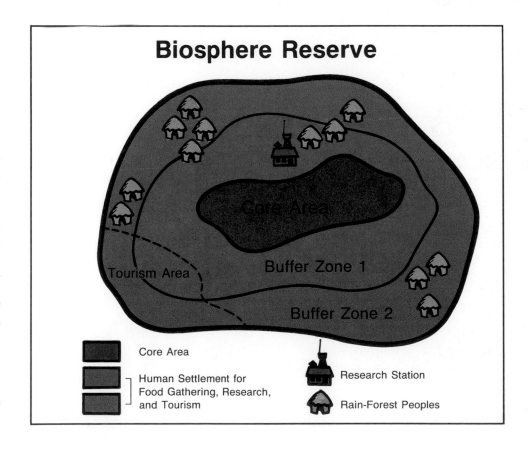

Biosphere Reserve

Core Area

Tourism Area

Buffer Zone 1

Buffer Zone 2

Core Area

Human Settlement for Food Gathering, Research, and Tourism

Research Station

Rain-Forest Peoples

LEARNING TO LIVE TOGETHER
MAB in Madagascar

The large island of Madagascar lies east of Africa in the Indian Ocean. The eastern coast of the island contains tropical rain forests, where unusual animals and plants live. Some of these species—such as lemurs, chameleons, and flowers called periwinkles—can be found nowhere else in the wild.

Since the early 1900s, Madagascar's tropical rain forests have been disappearing rapidly. As the number of people on the island has increased, farmland and food have become scarce. Madagascar's people and developers have cut down the rain forests to provide food and foreign income. Small-scale farmers, for example, clear the rain forests to plant rice, which is an important part of the islanders' diet. Large-scale farmers raise livestock and grow cloves, coffee, and sugarcane, which are sold in international markets.

In the early 1990s, because of demands for farmland, the island had only one-fifth of its original rain forest left. Many of Madagascar's unique plants and animals have become extinct in recent decades because their habitat has shrunk.

To combat this problem, the United Nations' Man and the Biosphere (MAB) program set up a **biosphere reserve** in Madagascar. Not just a wildlife sanctuary, the reserve is a place where human beings can live in balance with nature.

People farm special zones in the MAB reserve without harming the soil or pushing the indigenous species farther toward extinction. In other zones, the animals and plants live and breed in safety. Madagascar's MAB reserve offers hope to this spectacular island, which is struggling to protect its people as well as its environment.

Chameleons inhabit Madagascar's MAB reserve. Members of the lizard family, these animals can rapidly alter the color of their skin in response to changes in light or temperature.

without destroying them or pushing their indigenous species toward extinction. MAB has set up more than 280 biosphere reserves in 72 different countries.

Individual governments often establish national and regional reserves and parks to protect the plants and animals within their borders. Worldwide, there are more than 3,500 national protected areas that are helping to preserve nearly a billion acres (400 million hectares) of habitat.

LAYING DOWN THE LAW

Overhunting by humans has pushed many species toward Extinction Cliff. A lot of countries now have laws against hunting, buying, and selling endangered animals and plants. In the 1800s, for example, hunters reduced populations of the Russian saiga, an antelope that lives on the steppes (grasslands) of Europe, Russia, and central Asia. By 1900, only several hundred members of the species remained. In 1919, the Russian government made a law forbidding people to hunt the saiga. Within

Sitting among illegally obtained skins and ivory, a ranger in Kenya holds the huge horn of an African rhino.

70 years, millions of these antelope again inhabited the steppes.

International concern about rapidly increasing extinctions led many countries to sign the Convention on International Trade in Endangered Species (CITES).

Members of CITES agree to stop or to limit the buying and selling of endangered plants and animals.

The agreement also governs the buying and selling of products made from endangered species. More than 100 countries have joined CITES, which protects about 20,000 endangered species, including cacti, orchids, leopards, and tortoises.

RAISING HOPE

Scientists sometimes try to stop the extinction of plants and animals by raising them in zoos and in botanical gardens (zoos for plants). The scientists hope that conditions in the wild will improve. The endangered species, although born or raised in captivity, could then be reintroduced to their native habitats.

Small fences protect unhatched turtle eggs at a wildlife center in Brazil. Animals and people often take so many of the eggs that, without the added protection, fewer turtles would be born.

SAVING THE CALIFORNIA CONDOR
A Captive-Breeding Story

Once upon a time, there were thousands of California condors flying free in coastal areas of North America. By the early 1600s, explorers were mentioning these large birds of prey in their descriptions of California. In the 1700s and 1800s, as more people settled and developed California's wilderness areas, the birds lost their habitat.

By 1967, the California condor was on the U.S. list of endangered species. By the early 1980s, chemical poisoning was threatening the few California condors remaining in the wild.

Throughout the 1980s, to combat the loss of the birds, researchers took chicks from condor nests and raised them in zoos. Zoo scientists also captured wild condors

Through captive breeding and reintroduction, the California condor is making a comeback in the wild.

for breeding. In 1987, a trap caught the last free-flying California condor. The world's total population of California condors—all in captivity—numbered 27.

Within a few years, the captive birds were laying several eggs annually. The number of birds had risen to more than 50 by 1991. In August of that year, two condors that had been born and raised in captivity were set free in a special wildlife reserve. Once again the California condor soared over coastal areas of North America.

This story does not yet have a happy ending, however. For a program like this to succeed, we need to protect existing habitats so that endangered species have a chance to live in their natural surroundings.

Wearing a radio collar and a blindfold, an Arabian oryx is reintroduced to the desert plains of Oman in the Middle East.

This idea will only work, however, if we restore the plant's or animal's natural home. If we continue to destroy habitats, **reintroduction** will fail.

One of the happiest stories of reintroduction concerns the Arabian oryx, a delicate deerlike animal that lives in the Middle East. Hunting nearly eliminated all the members of this animal species. In the 1960s, the WWF, the IUCN, and the Fauna and Flora Preservation Society successfully captured three wild oryx and put them with six captive members that were already in zoos.

These conservation groups then set up a breeding program in the southwestern United States. This hot, dry area probably seemed like home to the endangered animals. Over the next 20 years, the herd of healthy, thriving oryx grew in number. In the 1980s, wildlife experts began to reintroduce the animal into Israel, Jordan, and Oman. Today, the graceful Arabian oryx once again walks the dry plains of its native habitat.

A tree called *Sophora toromiro* once thrived on Easter Island in the South Pacific. In 1962, the last indigenous *Sophora toromiro* tree died. But a scientist had brought one specimen of the tree to a botanical garden in Europe. As a result, the *Sophora toromiro* did not become extinct. The tree—the last of its kind—still lives in captivity but no longer exists in the wild.

PROTECTION IS WORTH IT

In many poor areas of the world, populations are growing rapidly, but good farmland and food are scarce. Sometimes the way people live and care for their families puts pressure on endangered animals, plants, and habitats. Moreover, the people in rich countries often encourage the pressure by buying products that come from endangered species or habitats.

Maybe the only way members of an Indonesian family can obtain farmland is to clear and burn a piece of tropical rain forest near their home. The family's alternative

Within a short time, the oryx has adapted to its native habitat.

is to starve. Perhaps a man in Kenya needs the money from selling ivory tusks to send his children to school. His motive is to try to pull his family out of poverty. There might be a Brazilian man who captures tropical birds to sell as pets to increase the family's income. With that money, he can feed and clothe his children.

A vendor offers a pair of parrots for sale in Guatemala, Central America. In many cases, the birds die before they reach their new homes.

We need to find economic solutions that make it unnecessary for people in poor nations to use endangered species for food, shelter, and income. In addition, we need to remember that in some countries protecting species can require a drastic change in a traditional lifestyle. In India, for example, the government had to relocate the people in 33 villages to make protected areas for Operation Tiger. This move was difficult for villagers.

Some governments in tropical countries have established **extractive reserves.** In these protected areas, resident families can extract (collect) a certain amount of a rain-forest product, such as natural rubber or Brazil nuts, without hurting the rain forests.

Ecotourism has become a source of income for countries with endangered habitats, plants, and wildlife. People from wealthy nations pay money to visit carefully managed preserves, where species are on view in the wild. These ideas are helping local people to see that protecting indigenous plants and animals is worth it.

On an extractive reserve in Brazil, a Waiwai worker is able to live and gather food in the rain forest without damaging its fragile communities of animals and plants.

Visitors travel to many countries to see wildlife, such as this watchful leopard, in their native habitats. After killing its prey, a leopard usually drags it into a tree so that lions cannot share the feast.

CHAPTER SIX

WHAT CAN WE DO?

Luckily, we do not have to keep a three-toed sloth in the bedroom to help preserve our planet's endangered plants and animals. We can lend a hand in many practical ways to prevent extinctions and habitat losses and to improve the quality of life on the earth. How we behave and what we buy make a difference.

■ *BUY PRODUCTS THAT ARE COLLECTED WITHOUT HURTING ENDANGERED HABITATS, PLANTS, OR ANIMALS.* The fact that a product, such as a beauty aid or a food, supports preservation of endangered species and habitats is likely to be marked on the package.

■ *DON'T BUY PRODUCTS MADE FROM ENDANGERED PLANTS AND ANIMALS.* Encourage the people around you to follow this rule, too. Tropical timber species often end up as patio furniture, chopsticks, and cardboard boxes. Purchasing a tortoise-shell comb or a pair of ivory earrings contributes to the

(Left) A boy scout protects the sand dunes of northern Indiana by picking up litter. (Above) A U.S. company has added rain-forest nuts to a new flavor of ice cream. The nuts come from an extractive reserve in Brazil and show that, when protective methods are used, people can profit from rain forests without harming them.

permanent loss of species that sacrificed their lives to provide these products.

PROTECT NATIVE HABITATS. You may not have any endangered species in your neighborhood, but you can still improve conditions for the plants and animals that do live there. Pick up trash. Don't litter. Don't destroy local plants or animals.

REDUCE, RECYCLE, REUSE, DO WITHOUT. By using fewer resources, we reduce the need to destroy natural habitats to obtain more resources. If your school or community does not yet have a recycling program, ask a teacher or a parent to help you start one.

JOIN AND SUPPORT ORGANIZATIONS THAT PROTECT ENDANGERED ANIMALS AND PLANTS. Ask your nearest zoo if it has an "adopt-an-animal"

program for its endangered species. Get sponsors per mile for a ride-for-wildlife bike trip. Send the money you earn to an organization that works to protect habitats.

WRITE LETTERS. Let the people who make decisions know that you care about endangered species and habitats. Put pressure on the heads of your government, the leaders of international agencies, and local politicians to fund programs that save habitats and endangered plants and

Recycling as many products as we can—paper, aluminum, tin, plastic, glass, and cardboard— helps to reduce the amount of new materials we need to make.

RIDING ON THE WILD SIDE

In 1989, the kids in Ms. Bock's eighth-grade class at Lake Villa Intermediate School in Lake Villa, Illinois, were learning about endangered wildlife. The students decided they wanted to make a difference in the future of species that are at the brink of extinction. The big question was, HOW?

After some intense classroom discussions, the eighth-graders came up with the idea of a bike-a-thon to raise money to protect wildlife. The money would be sent to organizations that are directly involved in preventing the extinction of endangered species. By voting, the class chose its two favorite species—the mountain gorilla and the California condor.

Over a period of 18 weeks, the students formed committees to organize every part of the all-day bike-a-thon. They found sponsors who promised to pay the students a certain amount of money for each mile they biked. The eighth-graders persuaded local businesses to donate raffle prizes. They distributed flyers throughout Lake Villa so that residents would know the bike-a-thon's route. The group even got a sponsor to make T-shirts for the event.

On May 20, 1989, more than 100 students pedaled around a 2-mile [3.2 kilometer] course and eventually logged about 2,000 miles [3,219 kilometers]. Their efforts raised almost $2,800 for the World Wildlife Fund and the National Wildlife Federation. As one participant said, "We hope [the bike-a-thon] encourages other people to see that even a small group can do something good."

A poster announces Lake Villa Intermediate's bike-a-thon.

These students are writing to national and international leaders to influence their decisions on the future of Antarctica.

animals. Remind these leaders of the human actions that contribute to the loss of species. Public libraries usually have the addresses you will need.

LEARN MORE ABOUT THE WEB OF LIFE AND OUR PLACE IN IT. Choose an endangered species and read about its habitat and relationship to other species. Study the influence of people on the species and then share your knowledge with others.

A young girl closely studies her pet turtle. Learning more about the wildlife, plants, and habitats around us can lead to a lifelong commitment to preserving our planet's diversity and resources.

ORGANIZATIONS

CENTER FOR PLANT CONSERVATION
Missouri Botanical Gardens
Post Office Box 299
St. Louis, Missouri 63166

GREENPEACE
1436 U Street
Washington, D.C. 20009

NATIONAL AUDUBON SOCIETY
666 Pennsylvania Avenue SE
Washington, D.C. 20003

THE NATURE CONSERVANCY
1815 North Lynn Street
Arlington, Virginia 22209

U.S. FISH AND WILDLIFE SERVICE
Department of Training and Education
4401 North Fairfax Drive
Arlington, Virginia 22203

**WORLD WILDLIFE FUND/
CONSERVATION INTERNATIONAL**
1250 24th Street NW
Washington, D.C. 20037

THE WILDERNESS SOCIETY
900 17th Street NW
Washington, D.C. 20006

Photo Acknowledgments

Photos are used courtesy of: p. 1, Steve Brosnahan; p. 4, NASA; p. 6, © Gerry Lemmo; p. 8, MPLIC; p. 9 (top), Center for Afghanistan Studies; pp. 9 (bottom), 59 (top), WWF; p. 10, James H. Carmichael; pp. 11, 66 (right), Hennepin County Library; p. 13, LeRoy G. Pratt; p. 14, © W. Ormerod/VU; pp. 16, 59 (bottom), 66 (left), IPS; p. 17, Puerto Rican Federal Affairs Administration; p. 18, Tim Krieger; p. 19 (left), Australian Overseas Information Service; pp. 19 (right), 23, AID; p. 20, Sawyer/WWF; p. 21, Kenneth W. Fink/Root Resources; p. 22, MN Dept. of Transportation; pp. 24 (left), 52, © Walt Anderson; p. 24 (right), American Lutheran Church; p. 25, Jerg Kroener; p. 26, © Gilcrease Museum, Tulsa, OK; p. 27, © Martin Harvey/The Wildlife Collection; p. 28 (left), Pete Carmichael; p. 28 (right), Moore/WWF; p. 29, National Association of Conservation Districts; p. 30 (left), Herbert Fristedt; p. 30 (right), John D. Cunningham/VU; p. 31, New Zealand Tourist and Publicity Office; p. 32 (left), Kay Shaw Photography; pp. 32 (right), 38 (bottom), David Falconer; p. 33, Edward S. Ross; p. 34, © David Julian; p. 35 (left), Phyllis Cerney; p. 35 (right), Sallie Sprague; pp. 37, 43 (right), Center for Plant Conservation; p. 38 (top), E. F. Anderson/VU; p. 39, © Brian Hawkes/NHPA; p. 40, © Saul Mayer; 41 (inset), Richard A. Fridell; p. 42, Mattias Klum/WWF UK; p. 43 (left), Philippine Dept. of Tourism; p. 44, Schmieder/WWF; p. 45, Lovett/WWF; p. 46, Minneapolis Athenaeum/Patricia Drentea; p. 47, Falkland Islands Tourist Board; p. 48, Joe McDonald/VU; p. 50 (top left), Robert Fox/Impact Visuals; p. 50 (top right), Leonard Soroka; p. 50 (bottom), © Morgan/Greenpeace; p. 53, Gunther/WWF; p. 54, Thorsell/WWF; p. 55, D. Clendene/USFWS; pp. 56–57, Newby/WWF; p. 58, Roma Hoff; p. 60, Kitty Kohout/Root Resources; p. 61, Glenn Moody; p. 62, WI DNR; p. 63, Judith Bock; p. 64 (top), Patricia Drentea; p. 64 (bottom), © Lynn M. Stone; p. 67, © Robert Barber; p. 68, John Vryens; pp. 69–70, FAO. Charts and illustrations by pp. 12–13, 36, 41, Laura Westlund; p. 51, Bryan Liedahl.

Front cover: R. L. Herman/USFWS
Back cover: (left) Kitty Kohout/Root Resources; (right) James Mejuto

acid rain: rainfall that contains chemical pollutants from the air. When combined with water, these pollutants form acids that can harm plants, animals, and habitats.

adapt: to change to fit a new situation.

bacteria (bak-TEER-ih-yuh): very small, single-celled plants.

Chimpanzees belong to the scientific class Mammalia, which is one of eight classes of animals with vertebrae (backbones).

biodiversity (by-o-dih-VER-sih-tee): the many different kinds of living things in a natural habitat.

biosphere reserve: a conservation area that has an inner zone reserved for animal and plant habitats and surrounding outer zones that humans are allowed to use.

class: within the plant and animal kingdoms, the third category of scientific classification, ranking above the order and below the phylum or division.

This frog is part of the rich biodiversity of South America's tropical rain forests.

dichloro-diphenyl-trichloroethane (DDT): a chemical insect killer that easily becomes concentrated in the bodies of animals and plants.

diversity: variety.

division: within the plant kingdom, the second category of scientific classification, ranking above the class and below the kingdom.

ecotourism: money-earning programs that arrange carefully managed visits by tourists to fragile natural habitats.

endangered: a category used by conservationists to describe species that are in danger of becoming extinct and that are unlikely to survive if present conditions continue.

evolution: an ongoing process of change in a species.

extinct: no longer existing.

extinct species: an animal or plant that has not been seen in the wild in the past 50 years.

The bald eagle—the national bird of the United States —has been an endangered species since the 1970s.

extractive reserve: a protected piece of land from which workers can harvest products under careful management.

family: within the plant and animal kingdoms, the fifth category of scientific classification, ranking above the genus and below the order.

gene (JEEN): a part of a cell in which specific information for an inherited trait is stored. A gene transmits that trait from a parent to its offspring.

genetic diversity: the many different traits in the genes of a single species that enable it to adapt to new living conditions.

genus (JEE-nuhs): within the plant and animal kingdoms, the sixth category of scientific classification, ranking above the species and below the family.

habitat: a natural setting that provides the necessities of life for plants and animals.

Most gorillas sleep in burrows, which the animals form by scooping out a nest from the plants in their habitat.

A worker sprays a pesticide on a field in Senegal, West Africa, to get rid of tsetse flies.

indigenous (in-DIJ-ih-nuhs): naturally originating, growing, and reproducing in a particular region or environment.

kingdom: the first and largest category of scientific classification for plants and animals.

mammal: any animal with a backbone whose young are nourished with milk from the mother's body.

mutate (MEW-tayt): to change inheritable traits slightly but permanently over time.

order: within the plant and animal kingdoms, the fourth category of scientific classification, ranking above the family and below the class.

pesticide (PES-ti-side): a chemical used to kill insects or other pests.

poacher: a person who hunts wildlife illegally.

pollen: among seed plants, the fine dust that carries the male reproductive cells of new plants.

pollinate: to place pollen on a flower so that male cells can join with female cells to produce new plants.

phylum (FY-luhm): within the animal kingdom, the second category of scientific classification, ranking above the class and below the kingdom.

rare: a category used by conservationists to describe species with small but stable populations that require careful monitoring.

reintroduction: the process of returning a species that has become extinct or rare in the wild to its natural habitat after raising a few members in a zoo or special preserve.

species (SPEE-sheez): a kind of living thing. Within the plant and animal kingdoms, a species is the seventh—and most specific—category of scientific classification.

taxonomy: the science of naming and classifying living things.

terrestrial (teh-RES-tree-uhl): living on land.

vulnerable: a category used by conservationists to describe species that are less threatened than those in the endangered group but that are likely to move toward extinction if present conditions continue.

web of life: the complex interaction of all animals and plants, which supply food, shelter, and other needs to one another.

Lion cubs participate in the web of life as they feed on the carcass of an impala antelope.

INDEX